Your Two Brains

YOUR TWO BRAINS

by
Patricia Stafford

ILLUSTRATED
BY LINDA TUNNEY

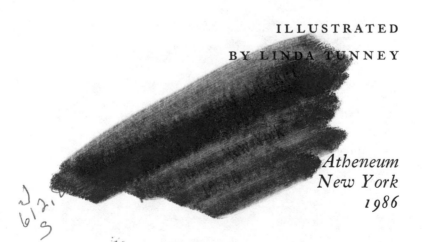

Atheneum
New York
1986

Special thanks to Fran Grace,
my balloonist friend,
for her help.

Library of Congress Cataloging-in-Publication Data

Stafford, Patricia.   Your two brains.

Bibliography: p. 69.
Includes index.
SUMMARY: A simple explanation of the separate function
of each half of the brain describing what each half does,
how they work together, and how one can achieve
whole brain thinking.
1. Cerebral dominance—Juvenile literature.
2. Brain—Localization of functions—Juvenile literature.
3. Intellect—Juvenile literature. [1. Brain—
Localization of functions. 2. Intellect] I. Tunney, Linda, ill.
II. Title. III. Title: Your 2 brains.
QP385.5.S73   1986   612'.825   85-28575
ISBN 0-689-31142-7

Published simultaneously in Canada by
Collier Macmillan Canada, Inc.
Type set by Heritage Printers, Charlotte, North Carolina
Printed and bound by Fairfield Graphics, Fairfield, Pennsylvania
Designed by Mary Ahern
First Edition

With love to my children,
Michael, Teresa, Marie, and Stephen;
and my grandchildren,
Christine, Jennifer, Kerry, Antony, and Philip.
And to my friend and advisor,
Ross Olney.

ACKNOWLEDGMENTS

This book could never have been a reality without the encouragement of loving family and friends.

My thanks to:
Pat, Alice, Winny and Anita, Joe, Marion and Frank,
Judy and Ed, Gloria, Florence, and JB.

Cathy and Keith Case for their creative suggestions.

Linda Martinez for her expert assistance.

Betty Edwards, Madeline and Rob Hunter, Barbara
Coloroso, Roger Taylor, Phyllis Wood, and Billie Telles
for the inspiration I received from their lectures.

Lyn Perino, Dr. James Cowan, and Steve Kingsford for
their moral support.

My editor, Marcia Marshall, for her interest and
cooperation.

CONTENTS

Your Two Brains

I
Your Brain

"QUIET!"

"Shush!" whispered voices in the dark. Suddenly the door opened and a young figure entered the dark room.

"Surprise! Surprise!" shouted many excited voices. On went the lights to reveal colorful balloons and bright crepe paper streamers decorating the room. A group of children moved forward. Each one carried a brightly wrapped gift.

"Happy birthday to you! Happy birthday to you! Happy birthday, dear Kerry! Happy birthday to you!" sang the young voices.

Not one of this group of children was enjoying the surprise party one bit. Not one of them could really walk, talk, smile, or sing. Not without help. They were just a group of puppets on a stage. There wasn't a brain in a single head. All the puppets' actions were controlled by real children. These children *did* have brains. Their brains made it possible for them to move the strings and make the sounds so that the puppets could perform.

Without a brain you, too, would be like a puppet. You wouldn't be able to laugh, cry, talk, or move. In fact, you wouldn't have any feelings at all. You would have no idea what was going on in the world around you.

Our brains are perhaps the most wonderful, magical exciting objects in the world. They are so complex that even the best scientists have barely begun to understand all there is to know about how they work.

A long time ago people believed that all real thoughts and feelings came from the heart. Today we know that the brain is the center of our being. It is what makes you the person that you are. You think with your brain. With it you can decide what is beautiful or ugly and what is good or bad.

Your feelings of pain and sadness, joy and laughter come from your brain. Your brain makes it possible for you to speak and understand words. It allows you to laugh at a funny story, solve problems, and remember events that happened to you a long time ago. Sometimes it makes you daydream and imagine wonderful adventures.

Your brain controls all your actions, thoughts, and feelings. It is made up of ten billion nerve cells and is a part of your central nervous system. There are three main parts: the CEREBRUM, the CEREBELLUM, and the BRAIN STEM. And each part has its own special job to do.

Cerebrum

The cerebrum is about the same size as a softball, but it is much heavier. It weighs about three pounds and is about seventy percent of our total brain. It is made up of many wrinkled folds. In fact, it looks something like the kernel of a walnut. However, instead of being hard and brown, it is soft, jellylike, and pinkish gray. Push your fingers against your forehead. The cerebrum is located right behind your skull bone and fills the whole upper part of your head inside your skull.

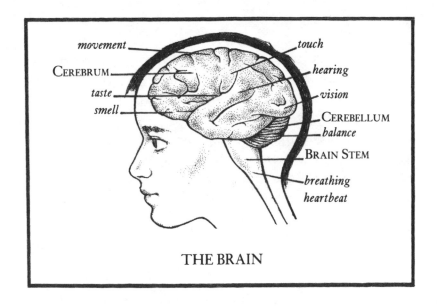

THE BRAIN

Your thoughts and being aware of what goes on around you come from your cerebrum. It controls what you learn and remember by processing and storing information. Some of your movements and all your senses (touch, smell, hearing, taste, and sight) are controlled by the cerebrum.

The cerebrum has two halves connected together by nerves. This connection is called the corpus callosum. Each side of the cerebrum controls the opposite side of your body by the nerves that cross from one side to the other. If you stamp your left foot, the right side of your cerebrum sends the message for your foot to do this. And, if you raise your right arm, that action will be controlled by the left side of your brain.

The surface of the cerebrum is called the cerebral cortex. It is a thin layer of nerve cells that protect the cerebrum as bark protects a tree. If you look up the meaning of the word "cortex" in a dictionary, you will see that it means "bark." The cortex is the wrinkled part of the cerebrum. If it were stretched, it would cover more area than a pillow case. The rest of the cerebrum consists of soft tissue nerve fibers called white matter.

The cerebrum acts as a storehouse for our intelligence and skills. The functions and actions of this part of our brain are what make it possible for human beings to do so much more than animals can. You will learn more about the cerebrum functions in Chapter Two.

Cerebellum

The cerebellum is about ten percent of our brain. It is about the size of an apple and is located behind and below the cerebrum. It, too, is made up of white matter with an outer layer of gray matter. It is even more wrinkled than the cerebrum.

Do you like to swim, play baseball, skate, or play arcade games? These are some of the many activities that the cerebellum helps you do. It controls your balance and coordination. It does this by means of a complicated, but very precise, network of nerve cells (or neurons). These neurons send strong signals to different parts of your body.

To control your muscle movement the cerebellum receives information from many areas of your body: from the eyes and ears; from receptors (a group of cells that receive messages) in your muscles and joints; and from the cerebral cortex. The cerebellum puts all the information together to make your body move in just the right way. It helps make it possible for you to play games and do other activities that take physical skill. If the right signals weren't sent to your body from the cerebellum, you would not be able to run, dance, or play a musical instrument. In fact, it would not be possible for you to walk across the room without stumbling or to talk without mumbling.

Brain Stem

Your brain stem is the widened top of your spinal cord. It is at the base of your skull just below the cerebellum and is about eight centimeters long. That is a little longer than a pencil before it has been sharpened. The lower and most important part of the brain stem is the medulla. Your heart would not beat and you could not breathe properly without the medulla. It regulates these functions and many other things you do every day without thinking about them. You

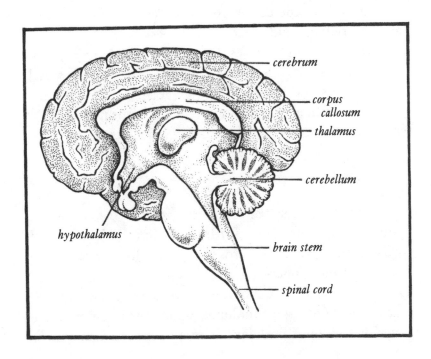

could not swallow, digest food, cough, sneeze, or blink your eyes without the help of the medulla.

Another important function of the brain stem is the control of consciousness. It switches the activity of the brain off and on again as we sleep and wake. That doesn't mean that our brains stop working when we are asleep. It just means that different activities are going on.

Growing out of the brain stem are several small parts of the brain. One, called the thalamus, receives signals from your senses. It can feel pressure, pain, hot, and cold. For example, suppose you were to step on a sharp tack. The thalamus will send a message to the cortex which will let you know where you hurt and why. The thalamus also controls your sleep and your good and bad feelings.

Another small brain part is called the hypothalamus. It has the important job of controlling your emotions. The hypothalamus is the center for your feelings such as fear, hunger, tiredness, and worry.

All information comes into your brain along the nervous system and is constantly being checked and monitored by the brain stem. Like a computer, it sorts out all this information. It then sends messages back into the nervous system, which controls the entire body and all its actions.

Spinal Cord

Although the spinal cord is not actually a part of the brain, it is very important for brain functions. Your spinal cord extends about two-thirds of the way down your back.

Run your fingers up and down the middle of your back. You will feel knobby bones, which are called vertebrae. This is your spinal column, which forms a protective covering for your spinal cord. The spinal cord is a bundle of nerves that run down the inside of the spinal column. A network of nerves then branches from the spinal cord to all parts of your body. Your body makes use of this network when it carries the messages to and from various parts of the brain.

All the parts of this amazing brain of yours work something like a combination of a gigantic telephone switchboard, television network, and a complex computer. However, no switchboard, television, or computer exists that has the billions of connections found in the human brain. There is just nothing on earth that can compare with the performance of your fantastic brain.

2
The Two-Sided Brain

A WORLD WAR II soldier named W.J. threw himself on the floor. His body twisted and turned. His head, arms, and legs jerked in every direction. His eyes rolled in his head. His mouth was foaming. "What can we do for him?" the nurse asked. "The poor man must be in agony."

"Yes, his is the worst case of epilepsy we've ever had. These fits come on several times a day," replied the doctor.

"Do you know anything about his history?"

"W.J.'s story is a sad one," the doctor answered. "During the war he parachuted from a plane and landed behind enemy lines. He was taken prisoner and sent to a prisoner of war (POW) camp. One day in the camp, when he was slow to obey an order, the butt of a rifle was smashed into his head with brutal force. The brain injury he received at that time has caused him to have these epileptic seizures. Normal life is impossible for him. We've tried every way we know to help him, but nothing has worked. I'm afraid we'll have to take some drastic action."

Not long after this, special brain surgeons decided to perform a new kind of operation on W.J. This was the only way they could think of to try to help him. In the operat-

ing room, the doctors cut the corpus callosum, the bridge that joined the two sides of W.J.'s brain. Their idea was to keep the violent nerve reaction from spreading back and forth from one side to the other. Perhaps this would limit the fits to only one side. It worked. It worked even better than they had expected. W.J. no longer had *any* seizures. He did, however, have problems with tasks that needed messages to go from one side of the brain to the other. When the corpus callosum is cut, one side of the brain cannot send messages to the other. The person has two separate minds working alone. One side has no idea what the other side is doing.

Doctors tested W.J. by asking him to raise his hand. Each time he was asked to do this he always raised the right hand. His left-brain understood the words, but it couldn't send the message to the other side of the brain to raise the left hand. Remember that each side of the brain controls the movements of the opposite side of the body.

W.J.'s operation was the first "split-brain" surgery. Since that time many more people have been helped by this operation. A large number of them have been children who suffered from epilepsy.

Now for the first time it was possible to find out things about the brain that had never been known before. By testing these "split-brain" people, doctors and scientists learned much more about the functions of our "two-sided" brain. They learned which tasks were usually performed by the left hemisphere and which by the right hemisphere.

Pretend that you can look down from the top of your head through your hair, scalp, and skull to your brain. You would see a soft, wrinkled, jellylike, pinkish-gray cerebrum, the largest part of your brain.

Now, look a little closer and you will see a deep valley

splitting the cerebrum in half. Below the valley the two halves are joined by a thick bridge. This bridge is called the corpus callosum. It is made of over two hundred million nerve fibers. This is the bridge that was cut in W.J.'s operation.

The two halves of your brain are called hemispheres. The two hemispheres are joined together, but they are like two people living in the same head, who act and think very differently. In ninety-five to ninety-seven percent of all people, the left hemisphere is the logical one and the right hemisphere is creative. There are some exceptions that will be explained later in this book.

Doctors have also tested many people who have had brain injuries or damage to only one side of the brain. These studies have added much to what we know about the right and left brain functions. Scientists' research has led them to believe that each of the two halves of our brain has its own special job to do, and each has its own way of doing them.

One hundred years ago it was discovered that our speaking and writing abilities came from the left brain in most people. Now we know that, in addition to reading, talking, and writing, our left brain also does basic mathematics. It sees everything in parts rather than looking at the whole. It puts things in order and categories. It is good at remembering people's names. It comes up with logical answers to problems. The left side does everything step by step. The left brain loves a game of chess or checkers.

Your left brain is kept very busy when you are in school. You use it when you read, memorize your spelling, write a story, learn your multiplication tables. It also remembers the sequence of events in social studies and learns step by step experiments in science.

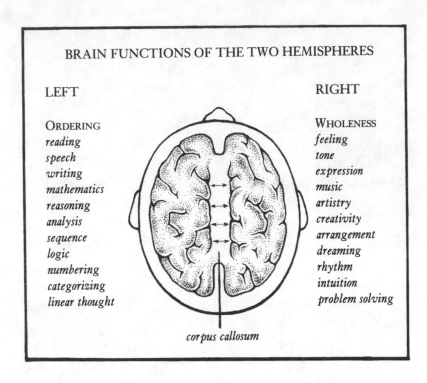

BRAIN FUNCTIONS OF THE TWO HEMISPHERES

LEFT	RIGHT
ORDERING	WHOLENESS
reading	feeling
speech	tone
writing	expression
mathematics	music
reasoning	artistry
analysis	creativity
sequence	arrangement
logic	dreaming
numbering	rhythm
categorizing	intuition
linear thought	problem solving

corpus callosum

The right brain is very different. It is artistic and creative. It is visual and sees things as a whole rather than in parts like the left brain. It gives you an understanding of location and direction. The right brain loves art, colors, and shapes. It also enjoys music. It is good at recognizing people's faces. It can think up great new ideas to solve problems, but it is not able to read, talk or write. It cannot put its great ideas into words by itself. The right brain loves jigsaw puzzles and mazes.

MARIE'S CAT didn't show up for several days. All the family was worried and was sure it was lost. But not Marie. "I just know Tiger will come back," she said. "I have a very strong feeling about it, a gut feeling. I can't explain it in words. I'm just sure that I'll have him back again."

Marie was using another right brain function called intuition. Intuition is knowing something that is based on an inner feeling, no on logic or reasoning. Intuition is sometimes right and sometimes wrong. But in Marie's case, her feeling was right. Her cat showed up the next day.

Mrs. Jones had a stroke that damaged her LEFT brain. She had trouble moving her right arm and leg. The whole right side of her body was partially paralyzed because the LEFT brain controls the movement of the RIGHT side of the body. Mrs. Jones could no longer talk or write. She had trouble remembering her friend's names. Talking, writing, and remembering names are all jobs of the left brain. One strange thing was that she could still sing and even sing the

words to songs. Somehow the music skills of rhythm and melody, which come from the right brain, had also made it possible for her to sing words.

Mr. Smith was in an automobile accident. The RIGHT side of his head was badly injured. His body became numb on the left side. He could still talk, but he had very little expression in his voice. He talked in what is called a monotone. He couldn't figure out how to put his clothes on. He couldn't find his way to the bathroom. The right brain sees things as a whole and is needed to do these tasks.

We do know what are the functions of the average person's right and left brain. But there have been times when persons who had an injury to the right or left hemisphere have overcome the problem. Strangely enough, in these cases, the other side takes over and learns to do all the things the injured side can no longer do. How some people's brains do this is still a mystery.

Genie, a thirteen-year-old girl, was found after she had spent most of her life completely alone. She was kept locked in a closet most of the time and was punished when she made any kind of noise. Because of this, she had not learned to talk or understand words. The left (verbal side) of her brain had not developed as it should. After Genie was found, she was taken away and placed in a kind, pleasant atmosphere. She was talked to in kind and gentle words. It took almost two years, but by the end of that time, she began slowly to speak and understand what was said to her. Her brain had the ability to overcome the damage that had been caused. It was a surprise to many that she was able to learn these things when she had spent so many years without using her brain.

Tony was searching for his lost dog. He went farther from home than he had ever been and he was lost. It would

be getting dark soon and he wanted to get home quickly. He had no idea where he was. Everything looked strange ... suddenly his right brain took over. It began to remember all the colors, sizes, and shapes of buildings he had passed. He began to get a feeling or intuition about what way to go. Then the left brain helped too. It began to read the street signs and remember the order of the streets in the town. Thanks to his "two-sided" brain, Tony made it home before dark. And his dog was waiting there for him. How the dog found his way home we don't know; but dogs are good at that.

It is generally believed that both sides of our brain always work together, but we don't know for sure. It is possible that instead of working exactly at the same time, they may have taken turns. They may even have fought each other for the controls. It's possible that the strongest side won the fight and did the job alone. Often one half of our brain is stronger than the other, but even so there is a constant stream of messages going back and forth between the two hemispheres. Each nerve fiber in the corpus callosum can fire about twenty messages per second. With millions of nerve fibers in the corpus callosum, each second four billion messages can be sent.

There are very many more things about the brain that remain a mystery. In the last quarter of this century more has been discovered about how our brains work than was ever known before. There is still much to learn and the scientists and doctors are finding out new things every day.

The old saying "Two heads are better than one" has taken on a new meaning.

3
Do You Prefer
the Right or
the Left?

WHEN you were born, your corpus callosum, that bridge between the right and left brain, was not fully developed. Because of this all your actions of seeing, hearing, and learning came from both sides of your brain. Your two hemispheres were both alike. By the time you were two or three years old the two sides had developed their own specific tasks. One side of your brain may also have become better than the other at doing certain jobs.

As you grew older you began to learn to read, write, and do arithmetic, which helped make the left brain stronger. You may also have spent time with such things as music lessons, art projects, and sports. These all helped to strengthen your right brain. The fact that the left and right sides of the brain become stronger after performing these specific kinds of tasks is true for at least ninety-five percent of the population.

All people, unless they have had brain damage, have ability to use the right and left hemispheres of their brain. We do, however, have a tendency to be either more right-

or more left-brained. This is called a "brain preference." Some people will have a fairly equal balance of both sides. How about you? Try this easy test to find out about yourself.

Test Directions, Part 1:

On a large sheet of paper write the numbers 1 through 14 down the left side of the page. Read the questions in the book quickly and then choose the A or B answer that comes closest to your feelings or actions. Write the A or B next to the number on your sheet of paper. If there are any you cannot decide quickly, that's OK. Just skip them.

Test, Part 1:

1. Imagine that you are getting ready to put on your shoes and socks. Which sock would you put on first?
   A. Right   B. Left

2. You are having a problem with a situation at school. Would you be more likely to:
   A. Think about, and maybe write down, all the ways you can think of to solve it, then choose one.
   B. Wait to see if the problem will go away.

3. It is a rainy afternoon. Would you rather:
   A. Work on a model.   B. Do a crossword puzzle.

4. You have an hour to wait for a friend to come to your house.
   Would you rather:
   A. Read a good book.   B. Lie on your bed and daydream.

5. You are giving a party for your friends tomorrow. When you get up in the morning will you:
   A. Make a mental picture in your mind of all there is to do.
   B. Make a list of all the things you must do.

6. Which is the closest to a description of your room at home:
   A. Well organized with shelves, boxes, and drawers where certain types of things are kept in their special place.
   B. The casual look with a mixture of many types of things kept in different places.

7. When asked by a friend to tell what you did on vacation, do you:
   A. Easily talk about many things that happened.
   B. Say, "Oh nothing much."

8. When you ask someone how to get to their house, would you rather:
   A. Have them draw you a map.
   B. Have them explain it in words.

9. Your class is going on a field trip to a big city. Would you rather:
   A. Visit the government buildings in that city and learn about the different government jobs that take place there.
   B. Attend a class at the art museum to learn how to make puppets.

10. Your parents are giving a party. To help them get ready would you rather:
   A. Fix a flower arrangement.

B. Count out the number of forks, knives, and spoons needed.

11. When you are given a school project, would you rather:

A. Do it alone.   B. Work with a group.

12. Holding your pencil perpendicular to the floor (the pencil point will be pointing to the floor or ceiling), with the pencil at arm's length, directly in front of you, line it up with a door or windowframe, or edge of a chalkboard. While holding that position:

    A. Close your right eye. Did the pencil appear to move?

    B. Close your left eye. Did the pencil appear to move?

13. Your English teacher is going to give you homework. Would you rather she asked you to:

    A. Write a short story about yourself.

    B. Write a poem about yourself.

14. If you were asked to put together a new toy wagon, would you:

A. Count all the parts and follow the directions step by step.

B. Take a quick look at the diagram and then just go ahead and put it together without following the exact directions.

Test Directions, Part 2:

Now look at Part 2 of the test. You will see a list of things with letters next to them from *a* through *t*. On the right side of your paper make a column of *only* the letters that are next to something you enjoy.

Test, Part 2:

a. Drawing
b. Dancing
c. Collecting things
d. Swimming
e. Fishing
f. Playing cards
g. Bicycling
h. Scrabble
i. Video Games
j. Chess or checkers

k. Soccer
l. Discussing
m. Baseball
n. Hiking
o. Sewing
p. Reading
q. Jigsaw puzzles
r. Oral reports
s. Making party decorations
t. Word find puzzles

Scoring:

Now score your test. Match the answers on your paper with the SCORING KEY. Mark an R or L next to each one of the answers on your sheet. Next count the number of R's you have and the number of L's. Now what does it all mean? If you have the same number of each, your brain is probably rather evenly balanced. The further apart your two total numbers are, the more "brain preference" you have for one side or the other. For instance, if you have nine Rights and ten Lefts, you do not have a very strong preference. However, if you have fourteen Lefts and only five Rights, you can see what side of your brain is the strongest and which you prefer to use most. Having a "brain preference" to the right or to the left does not make you any better or worse than someone else. It is how we use our brains that count.

Scoring Key:

PART 1:

1.	A-Left	B-Right
2.	A-Left	B-Right
3.	A-Right	B-Left
4.	A-Left	B-Right
5.	A-Right	B-Left
6.	A-Left	B-Right
7.	A-Left	B-Right
8.	A-Right	B-Left
9.	A-Left	B-Right
10.	A-Right	B-Left
11.	A-Left	B-Right
12.	A-Left	B-Right
13.	A-Left	B-Right
14.	A-Left	B-Right

PART 2:

a.	Right	k.	Right
b.	Right	l.	Left
c.	Left	m.	Right
d.	Right	n.	Right
e.	Left	o.	Left
f.	Left	p.	Left
g.	Right	q.	Right
h.	Left	r.	Left
i.	Right	s.	Right
j.	Left	t.	Left

4
Boys and Girls, How Their Brains Differ

WHEN your grandparents were young, it was taken for granted and even encouraged that boys did "boys' things" and girls did "girls' things." Boys were expected to be active and play rough games. Girls were encouraged to be quiet and gentle. They were told to be "ladylike."

Children have always been influenced by their parents and others to do only certain things or to learn only some things. For example, a father may have said to his son, "Let's get out of the house, Philip, and play some ball. Then you can help me work on the car."

But if Philip's sister wanted to come along, she would have been told "No Jenny, you'll get your dress dirty. Why don't you read the book you got from the library. Your mother can use your help with the dinner, too." Philip was encouraged to be physical and mechanical while Jenny was praised for being a good reader and for her household skills.

In most cultures, boys were encouraged to be physical and mechanical, while girls were expected to be gentle and unaggressive.

Things have changed. Today you are "free to be you" no matter what your sex. Girls are active and enjoy sports. Boys are comfortable cooking or quietly reading a book.

Years ago, the jobs people had were also very limited by a person's sex. Only men held jobs as policemen, firemen, mailmen, doctors, lawyers, and plumbers. Women, if they worked outside the home at all, were usually teachers, librarians, nurses or secretaries.

Today you can choose what you want to be, what you have a talent for and what you are interested in. There are now women doing almost every type of job. There are many men who are now teachers, librarians, nurses, and secretaries.

But what about our brains? Do boys' and girls' brains really differ?

Remember, the results of scientific tests only give an average. Brain tests on boys and girls will only give us a general idea of some differences. They do not make allowances for the special talents that make each of us unique. Some girls and boys may show different results than the brain test averages show.

Brain scientists who have tested boys and girls have discovered that, in general, the brain size and functions of boys are different than that of girls.

When tested, girls have more manual dexterity. This means they can handle small items more easily with their fingers. There is also a difference in the way boys and girls solve problems. Boys generally pay more attention to rules and may try harder and longer to get an answer. Girls may not pay as close attention to the problem, but they are, however, good at gathering important facts faster.

Two differences in boys and girls that show up most often are: girls are usually the talkers and writers; boys usually take action. For example, on a school project the girls would be the ones who discuss what to do and the boys would build the models.

Boys are more interested in shapes, patterns, and colors. They are usually more mechanical and have a good sense of direction. Boys may be better at maps, mazes, and math.

Girls excel at all the skills that require words; reading, writing, talking. They are usually more sensitive and enjoy quieter activities.

Have you ever been present at a birthday party for five-year-old girls, or one for five-year-old boys? If you had been to one of each, you would have certainly seen a difference in how the boys and girls acted. You may have

watched the game of "Pin the Tail on the Donkey." Girls will calmly and quietly watch a player try to place the tail where it belongs. Boys are apt to push, shove, and shout. They may make it almost impossible for the boy whose turn it is to reach the target.

We don't know for sure why boys' and girls' brains are generally different. The influence of culture and how boys and girls have been treated may be one of the reasons. Scientific tests have shown, however, that differences in boys' and girls' brains appear very early in life.

Hundreds of tests on babies tell us there are differences from birth. Male babies usually watch and are more curious about lights, patterns, and objects. They like to handle objects and explore things. Female babies respond more often to people and are more interested in faces than objects.

They pay closer attention to people's voices. A mother's voice can calm a crying baby girl much easier than a baby boy. It has been shown that girl babies make more sounds than boys.

Most brain scientists think that the differences between boys' and girls' brains from birth are due to certain cell arrangements and chemicals in their bodies even before they are born.

Girls' brains at birth seem to be more fully developed. The corpus callosum, which connects the two brain hemispheres, is larger in girls. This makes it easier for girls to use both sides of the brain from the beginning. Boys receive more messages in the right brain and become more skilled in right-brained tasks, such as grasping objects. Girls more often use the left-brain skills, with help from the right brain as well.

All girls and boys will not follow these examples. Some girls are very athletic or good at mechanical tasks. There are many boys who have quiet natures or may be very good at creative writing.

Up until a child is about four or five years old, the corpus callosum is not fully developed in boys or girls. At this stage, they have a fifty-fifty chance to be either left- or right-brained.

One explanation of brain differences in sexes is that through the process of human development, brains have adapted to human needs. When the first people lived on earth (and for ninety-nine percent of all human history) they were called "hunter-gatherers."

Imagine yourself back in the time of the caveman. If you were a man or older boy, you would have been expected to hunt for food. To be a good hunter you would need to use the right brain function of the eyes. You would

have to be very strong and determined. Judging distances and being aware of direction would have been important, also. These are the same abilities that tests have shown boys are born with today.

If you were a girl or woman during those times, you would have had different tasks to perform. You would have taken care of small children and prepared the food that the hunters brought to you. It would have helped you to have a gentle and quiet nature. You would have used your hands to make clothing and cooking and eating utensils. It would not have been necessary for you to be strong. A cave woman or girl would have needed to be sensitive to emotions, sounds, and odors. In order to protect the children, you would have reacted quickly to sounds of danger. You would also have developed communication skills that men and boys did not need as much. These abilities, which are more evenly divided between the right and left brain, are what most girls are born with today.

There are many studies still being done on the differences between girls' and boys' brains. There is still much more for us to learn from research in this area.

None of these scientific findings means that boys are better than girls, or that girls are superior to boys. Both boys and girls process information and react to it, but generally in slightly different ways.

5
Left-Handed People

THE YEAR was 1930. The place, a small town school with three classrooms. In each room twenty-five or thirty students were busy doing handwriting exercises.

"Jimmy, get that hand down," one teacher shouted. In her classroom Jimmy and two other children had been told to sit on their left hands during this lesson.

In another room three students had their left hands tied behind their backs. They did not look happy.

In the third classroom, the teacher was walking up and down the aisles watching the students write. Once in a while she would hit Ed or Judy on the left hand with a ruler.

These classroom scenes may seem strange to you. However, in those days almost all teachers insisted that all pupils write only with their right hands. Even if they were naturally left-handed, they still were forced to write with the right hand. Each teacher had her own special way of dealing with the "problem."

Today, we know that to force left-handers to use the right hand can have some very bad effects. It can cause stuttering and other emotional problems. Now we allow students to use whichever hand they prefer for any task.

In 1932, it was thought that two percent of the world's population was left-handed. That was during the period when students were being forced to use their right hand. By 1970, a ten percent figure was given. Today, studies show that about fifteen percent or more of the people in the world are left-handed. In fact, this percentage has probably been true since the stone age.

Scientists have noted that the drawings found in prehistoric caves showed the people to be generally right-handed. Egyptian tombs also reveal almost all the figures doing tasks with their right hands. The few tools that have been found from early times indicate that they were made to be used by the right hand.

There was an interesting study of prehistoric baboon skulls that had been cracked. The location of these cracks in the skulls indicated that the baboons were probably killed by early humans with a club or other weapon held in the right hand.

We don't know why most people are right-handed.

Perhaps this hand became the strongest one in order to protect a man in battle. He held his spear in the right hand. This freed his left hand to cover his heart, which was located on the left side of his body. Later, when swords and shields were used, the shield was held by the left hand to cover the heart.

We usually don't know if a child is going to be right-handed or left-handed until they are over three years old. Before that time most children use both hands equally well.

There are about thirty-seven million Americans who are left-handed. There are almost twice as many males as females who have this trait. We are not sure why.

How about people who are left-handed? Is there anything wrong with using the left instead of the right? There has been a negative feeling and a prejudice against anything on the left side passed on through the ages. Associating left with "bad" has been with us for a long time. Even today if you look in a dictionary for the word "left," you will usually find at least one definition such as clumsy, insincere, or radical.

Today, we know that these old ideas have no truth to them. There is nothing bad about the left, or with being left-handed. In fact, as you will see later, it can often be an advantage.

There is, in a few left-handers, a difference in how their brain works. As you have learned before, the left brain in most people controls speech and writing, verbal tasks. The right brain controls physical as well as creative skills.

YOU MIGHT expect that left-handed people would simply have a crossover or reverse of right and left brain functions. However, this is not usually true. *About seventy percent of left-handers show the same brain patterns as right-handers.* Of the other thirty percent, half show speech control in the right hemisphere and half show speech coming from both the right *and* left hemispheres:

Seventy percent speech from left hemisphere.
Fifteen percent speech from right hemisphere.
Fifteen percent speech from both hemispheres.

So, as you can see, the majority of left-handers are no different than the right-handed person in brain activity.

Some scientists believe that the difference in these groups of left-handers is related to whether or not the left-

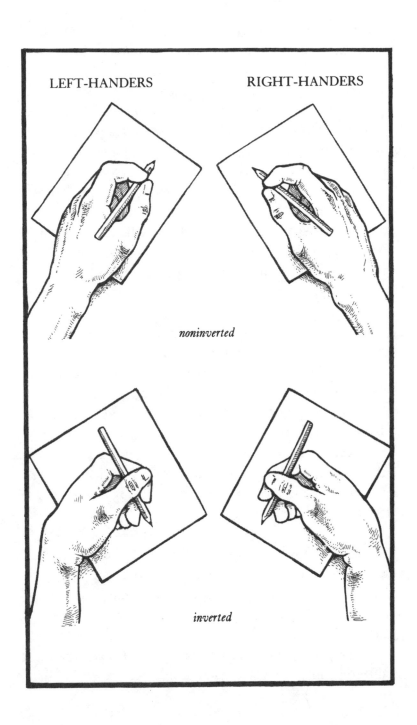

handedness is an inherited trait. Research shows that those who have no left-handedness in their family either have brain functions the same as right-handers or they show a crossover of some usual right and left functions. (For example some speech may come from both the right and the left brain.) Those left-handers *with* relatives who were or are left-handed show signs of speech coming entirely from the right hemisphere of the brain.

There is another trait that may help sort left-handers into different groups of brain organization. About sixty percent of left-handers write with their hand in a hooked position. They hold their pencil or pen above the line of writing. Other left-handers, as well as almost all right-handers, hold their writing instrument below the line of writing.

It is thought by some that the hand position gives a clue to which hemisphere is controlling speech. They feel that the left-hander with a hooked or inverted position has verbal functions from the left hemisphere. Those who hold their pencil or pen below the line of writing would have verbal skills from the right brain.

There are other scientists who do not agree with any of these findings. They feel that the environment (experiences with the family or school) may be a reason for these patterns.

"WHY ARE YOU so upset?" Frank's mother asked. "All you need to do is make a scrapbook for social studies."

"I know, but I get so mad every time I try to cut out pictures. Why can't you buy me some left-handed scissors?"

Some people who are left-handed feel that they must be different in some way. They don't need scientific facts to prove it. The difference is very clear. They have problems every time they use a pair of scissors, a pencil sharpener, a can opener, a pay phone, or take a picture with a camera. All these items are generally made to be used by right-handed people. (In recent years it has become possible to order certain left-handed tools and implements from special catalogs.)

LINDA, a left-hander, broke her left arm when she slid into home base during a ball game. For many weeks the broken arm was uncomfortable, but she managed very well doing the necessary tasks with her right hand. Her friend Lisa admired her ability. "Boy, if I ever break my *right* arm, I'd be in trouble. I can do hardly anything with my left."

Being left-handed has its advantages. These people, living in a world set up for right-handers, often find it necessary to use both hands. Therefore, they are likely to become ambidextrous (having the ability to use both hands with ease). Being skilled with both hands often results in superior right brain skills.

If you think of the left-handed people you know, you'd probably realize that some of them speak a great deal and *also* have artistic talents. This may be so because in order to adjust to a right-hand world, they often become quite talented in both brain hemispheres. Their speech skills often come from both sides of the brain.

Many great performers who are or were left-handed include: Judy Garland, Marilyn Monroe, Carol Burnett, Robert Redford, Michael Landon, Charlie Chaplin, Don Rickles, Rod Steiger, and Chuck Connors.

If you are left-handed, you have this in common with Presidents Gerald Ford, Harry Truman, Herbert Hoover, and Ronald Reagan. Also, some of the greatest and most creative geniuses such as: Ben Franklin, Albert Einstein, Pablo Picasso, Michaelangelo, and Leonardo da Vinci. They were all left-handed.

The attitude about left-handers has greatly changed through the years. Fifty or a hundred years ago, to be left-handed was considered to be wrong or bad. Believe it or not, some left-handed people were once considered to be witches. Today people can feel free to make use of whichever hand feels the most comfortable. Society has not only accepted left-handers; it also has recognized their special abilities.

6
Your Creative Brain

"ALBERT, will you please sit down at your desk and stay there," said the teacher. "Standing at the window is not where you should be."

"Albert, you haven't finished your Latin lesson or turned in an essay for days. If your attitude doesn't improve soon, I will have you expelled from this school."

Albert's attitude didn't improve and Albert *was* expelled. Albert's last name was *Einstein*.

Einstein was probably the most brilliant scientist the world has ever known. Because he was very ill as a child, he missed a lot of school. This caused problems with his language development. His other school problems were mostly because he was shy and dreamy and also a very visual person. In other words, he was "right-brained." He hated reading and the type of math and science he was taught in school. He loved to daydream. He would let his mind wander off, imagining all kinds of interesting fantasies and ideas.

After Einstein had become famous for his brilliant work in physics, one man asked him, "Dr. Einstein, how do you get some of your most original ideas?"

Einstein replied that he usually didn't think in words at all. "A thought comes, and I may express it in words afterwards," he said.

A surprising thing was, however, that in many of his other activities, he used words with no trouble. He liked to compose limericks and he wrote beautiful letters. This shows that he made good use of both sides of his brain. He had such a gift for creative ideas, though, that he more often used skills that did not require language. His great love of music and the violin and his deep spiritual beliefs indicate a strong right brain preference.

LET'S EXPLORE the creative right brain further.

The right brain sees everything as a whole. For example, because it understands location and direction, it can help you find your way around school and how to get back home. It actually makes a map in your mind of all the places you have been. This skill also helps you imagine or understand how mechanical objects work. When you play baseball, basketball, soccer, or tennis, it is your right brain that will help you win the game. When you look at a person's face, your right brain will allow you to see the whole face, not its parts. It will not help you to remember the person's name. The left brain will do that.

When you find yourself dreaming about other places, other times, or when your head is filled with ideas, thoughts, and fantasies, this is your imagination at work. This right hemisphere skill is also the one that creates new ideas and inventions.

The right brain uses intuition (hunches) and imagination to solve problems quickly. In contrast, the left brain uses logic or reasoning. The right brain creates new ideas to solve these problems. It tries many solutions until it finds the right one. It can also solve some types of problems by inventing mechanical objects.

Because of its powers of imagination, the right brain understands metaphors. (A metaphor is a figure of speech in which one thing is spoken of as if it were another.) The right brain will understand the real meaning behind this figure of speech. For example, "I have butterflies in my stomach," Terry said to Alice. Alice's right brain understood that there were not really butterflies in Terry's stomach, but that she was nervous about giving her oral report.

With its ability to understand a double meaning and to use imagination, the right brain gets the point of a joke. It is also quick to pick out the moral of a story and to understand the meaning of fables.

Your tone of voice and expression come from the right brain. Great actors are usually very right-brained.

They can be quite dramatic in their actor's role. Using their imaginations, they can actually believe themselves to be the person whose part they are playing. The left brain processes the words the actors are saying; but the right brain controls how those words are said.

Painting, drawing, woodcarving, and sculpting are examples of right brain artistic creativity. These skills also require imagination to create something original. The spatial skills of using a balance of line, color, and space are important to an artist.

"CHECK OUT that sunset!" Joe exclaimed. "Isn't it awesome?"

"Yes," Patty replied. "Look at those red streaks against the blue sky. I just love sunsets."

When a person enjoys looking at a sunset, a work of art, or a beautiful view, they are usually using their right hemisphere.

The ability to respond to music or rhythm is a right-brain function. (Although professional musicians who have studied a long time also rely heavily on the left brain.) When you sing, dance, enjoy listening to music, or play a musical instrument you are using this ability.

Ideas that seem to flash into your mind from nowhere are due to intuition. Have you ever said "I had a hunch," "I just knew you were coming," or "I was sure you would say that?" These are thoughts or intuitions that you can't explain in words; you just know. The right brain alone cannot put these feelings into words. Intuition, by itself, can sometimes mislead us. Our intuition may tell us one thing, but our logical left brain may not agree, and it may be right.

Meditation and prayer are types of spiritual thinking which generally use the right brain. Meditation is thinking deeply and continuously on a certain subject. Most cultures of the Eastern world (for example, Japan and India) place great value on meditation. They teach that it frees the mind and helps solve daily problems. Meditation and prayer are often called "mystical." Mystical thoughts use right-brain intuition rather than left-brain logic.

The right hemisphere of the brain is more in touch with feelings and emotions than the left. (Although your emotions actually come from a different part of the brain

called the limbic system.) Emotions can make you feel happy or sad, angry or afraid. The right brain can make you feel suspicious even when there is no logical (left-brain) reason for it.

Your body movements are generally controlled by the opposite side of the brain from the body part that moves. (Left brain controls *right* side of body. Right brain controls *left* side of body). However, the right brain has special control over movements on either side that require fast reaction time; actions such as in sports or video games.

"Creative" is the word most often used to describe the right hemisphere of the brain and right-brain activities. To create means to invent or make something from nothing. All of the great scientists, inventors, writers, artists, and musicians have become great due to their exceptional creative insights.

Mozart, a great musical genius, began composing when he was only five years old. At the age of six, he toured the capitals of Europe and played the piano, violin, and organ. He wrote his first symphony about this same time, and when he was twelve he wrote his first opera. Mozart was a master of melody and technique. To become such an accomplished musician, it took the creative powers of his right brain co-operating with the technical knowledge of the left. Often musical scores would flash into his thoughts out of nowhere. Later, he would hum the tune and add to it until he had a complete composition. Then he would finally write the notes on paper.

Even though Einstein was expelled from one school, he did go back and continue his education through high school and the university. No matter how creative he was, in order to be well balanced and achieve great success, it was necessary for him to develop and use both sides of his brain.

You aren't expected to be an Einstein, but as you can see, your right brain has fantastic mystical, magical powers— powers to help you accomplish great things in life. When your creative right cooperates with your logical left, who knows what wonderful things you will do?

7
Your Dreamy Brain

CHRISTINE was riding along a dark, winding road on a shiny new bike. It was hard to see through the wisps of thick fog that floated all around her. It was almost as if she was riding the bike blindfolded as she struggled so hard to see the road ahead. Slowly the fog began to clear, but she

now was no longer on a bike. Now she was walking through a shady forest and was feeling quite happy. Suddenly, from behind a large tree, leaped a fierce animal with sharp pointed teeth. She didn't know what kind of animal it was. Christine began to run fast. She was very frightened and could hear the animal coming closer. She looked back. The beast looked like a combination of a tiger, a fox, and a wolf. What she knew for sure was that it really looked fierce. Just as the animal was about to spring at her, Christine gave a giant leap and began to slowly rise up, up, up. She was actually floating through the air. She was flying. As she soared higher and higher, she could look down on the forest. The animal was nowhere to be seen. Now she really felt free as she glided up and down, back and forth, through the trees, over mountains, and through soft clouds. Christine was quite happy, but she had a strange feeling that nothing was real. Slowly her eyes opened. There she was in her bed, in her own room. "What a weird dream," she thought. "Scary, yes, but it really turned out OK."

Most of us have a dream like Christine's at one time or another. In the nighttime dream world it is quite common for people to change from one place to another, almost like magic. Sometimes you may be talking to one person and then you notice that they are not that person, but someone else. Often we are frightened by being chased by people, animals, or even monsters. The dream of flying, with a happy sense of freedom, comes to most everyone at some time. Some people enjoy dreams of flying over and over.

"I never dream," Winny told her daughter. "Oh, yes you do, Mom," Anita answered. "We learned in school that everyone has dreams, even small babies. You just don't remember them." Anita was right. Everyone does dream each night they go to sleep.

There are scientists who study dreams. Tests are taken by attaching electric wires to the scalp above the brain. From these tests it has been proven that everyone goes through several dream stages each night. Our eyes move around under our eyelids when we are dreaming. This is called Rapid Eye Movement (REM). When a person being tested is awakened during a REM period they can always describe their dream. People like Winny, who say they don't dream, or can't remember dreaming, are just not transferring their right brain dream to their left brain consciousness.

Do you ever have bad dreams? Most people do, particularly children. These bad, or frightening, dreams are called nightmares. Usually you will wake up just before something really bad happens to you, but you might still feel very upset. Some people know it is a dream even while the nightmare is going on.

Things can happen in our lives that cause us to have bad dreams at night. Even small disturbances can cause nightmares at times. Noises, such as thunder, lightning, and wind can disturb us. Sounds of cars, trucks, and trains can affect your dreams if you are sleeping in a strange place. Even barking dogs and yowling cats may cause your dream problems.

Dreams are mostly a right brain function. They are pictorial, not logical. They are unreal and emotional. Dreams are filled with fantasy and adventure. Your left brain seems to turn itself off when you go to sleep. A hidden, mysterious right brain effectively takes over. While dreaming, you are in a subconscious state. Subconscious means beneath the conscious.

When you remember things that have happened lately, lessons you have just studied, and people's names you see often, you are using your conscious mind. However, memories of *all* the things that have happened in your life are stored forever in your subconscious. The subconscious mind stores millions of bits of information something like a computer does. From this unconscious mind come many of these things of which we dream. They are often combined with recent events in our lives.

These nighttime adventures are almost like giant TV shows. At times you may be watching the TV screen and at other times you may be one of the actors. Do you dream in color? Some people do, but others say they only dream in black and white.

We don't fully understand why some dreams are often strange and unreal, like Christine's dream. But we know that people far back in history had weird and frightening dreams. Scientists are studying all these things. They hope to learn more about the purpose and meaning of these nighttime experiences.

IN A DENSE JUNGLE of a faraway land called the Malay Peninsula, live a group of people called the Senois. They are a primitive tribe of natives who are quite peaceful and also very creative. They, more than any group of people we know, are taught to understand and control their dreams.

A Senoi family is sitting in a circle, on grass mats before their early morning breakfast.

"What did you dream about last night?" the Senoi Chief asks his small grandson.

"Oh, I had a very bad dream," the boy reported. "A big, red, slinky snake was coming after me. He hissed and hissed and his sharp tongue flicked in and out. I ran as fast as I could. Just as he was about to grab me, I woke up."

"Child," the grandfather tells him, "next time you have a dream of someone or something chasing you, try not to run. Stop and face your enemy. Try to overcome your fear and danger. If you can't do this alone, find some friends in your dream to help you."

Every day from the time a child first begins to talk, all the children of this tribe are asked to share their dreams. Adults also discuss theirs with each other. By doing this they learn how to handle dream problems as well as everyday ones. They learn how to make themselves have the same dreams on other nights and change the endings. They have no trouble remembering dreams since they begin to practice this at a young age.

Senoi children learn three main things about their dreams; to face and control danger, to move toward pleasure in dreams (such as a flying sensation), and to always end dreams in a positive way. By practicing these things, this group of people have become famous for their happy and peaceful way of life. For over two hundred years, they have never had a really violent crime in or near their tribe.

It would be difficult for many of us to learn how to control our dreams like the Senoi. Dream specialists say that we can benefit by recalling our dreams and trying to understand some meaning behind them. One good way is to keep a "dream diary." Keep a notebook and pencil next to your bed. When you first awake in the morning, keep your eyes closed a moment and try to recall what you were just dreaming. Then write down as much as you can remember, even if it is just bits and pieces. When you are new at this, you may at first have trouble remembering. But if you keep trying day after day, it will become easier and soon you may remember whole dreams with very little trouble.

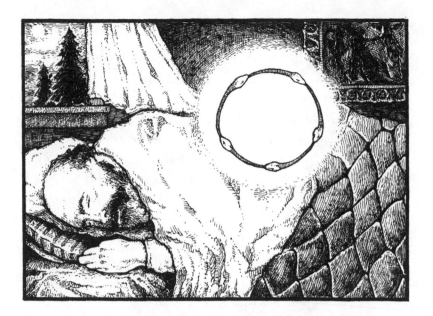

Many famous people have had great ideas while they were asleep. Musical composers, scientists, artists, and poets have all used ideas and solutions to problems that came to them in dreams.

In the nineteenth century, the scientist, August Kekule, was trying to find the chemical shape of a certain molecule (the Benegene molecule). He couldn't solve the problem. In his sleep he dreamed of snakes biting their tails. When he awoke, he realized that he had found the answer. This particular molecule had a circular shape. We may have in our unconscious brain many answers to problems and many new ideas. While we are dreaming with the active left brain turned off, the creative right can do wonders for us.

The meaning of a dream may be very confusing to you. Your dreamy right brain creates many fantasies and uses many symbols that are difficult to understand. It is filled with pictures and ideas. Don't worry if you can't understand your dreams at first. You might, after a while, find a pattern and some meaning to them. If you are still confused, don't let it bother you. Even the dream specialists who spend most of their time studying dreams have a very great deal more to learn.

It might be fun for you to see if you can change some of your bad dreams to have happy endings. Before you go to sleep try to think about pleasant endings or other things you want to happen in your dreams. You might be surprised at some of the creative ideas that come to you while you sleep. You may even solve some problems this way.

Another idea is to try to draw pictures of some of your dreams. This is particularly helpful if they are nightmares. Drawing them can "get it out of your system." Maybe these dreams won't come again.

One good reason to try to remember your dreams is that it helps to improve your ability to send information from the right to the left brain. This can be useful to you in many ways. Many of the subjects you study in school are mostly left-brained, but they can be greatly helped by your right brain. (One example would be to create a poem in your right hemisphere and then transfer to the left to put the words on paper.)

In addition to nighttime dreams we also have daydreams from time to time. Daydreams help us explore the world of our imaginations. They might be picturing in your mind all the wonderful places you would like to travel. Or they could be only about what you are going to do after school or what you want to have for dinner. They could also be imagining how things will be when you are grown up.

Daydreams, like nighttime dreams, usually come from your right hemisphere and can be creative. Einstein once daydreamed of riding on a moonbeam in space when he discovered the important theory of relativity.

In 1832, a small blond girl arrived in the United States from England at the age of eleven. Her name was Elizabeth Blackwell and she too had a dream. She daydreamed of many things she wanted to do to make this world a better place. But her greatest dream was to one day be a doctor. She was turned down by twenty-nine medical schools because she was a woman. There had never been a woman doctor in the United States. Eventually she was allowed to study at Geneva College, New York. In spite of much prejudice and criticism, she finally graduated at the head of her class. After much hard work, her dream did come true. She was the first woman doctor in the United States.

Even after she was a doctor, she had difficulty being truly accepted. She fought for her own right and that of other women doctors to practice medicine. She established her own hospital and medical school for women. Her advanced ideas of social hygiene and preventive medicine truly made her dream of making this world a better place come true.

Daydreaming can often be good for you. It can help you with creative ideas and with solutions to your problems, and it can also get in the way of other important learning. Daydreaming, at the right time and place, can enrich your life.

8

Put Your Brain to Work for You

"THE BRAIN is an organ of the body that starts working for you and doesn't stop until you get to school."

Of course this statement isn't really true; but, if it seems to be for you, there is something you can do about it.

Charles Schultz, the creator of the "Peanuts" comic strip, relies heavily on his right brain to come up with ideas. First, he puts himself in a relaxed mood and lets his imagination take over. He remembers different scenes and situations, usually from his childhood. Then, using his creative ability, he comes up with ideas for his comics. Some things he remembers are unhappy times or embarrassing moments when he was a small child. He is able to make these into wise and funny statements about life. When he does a cartoon, he sees the whole comic strip in his head at the same time (right brain). To get it down on paper, he must call on the left brain to help with the words and the step-by-step sequence of the drawings.

Schultz admits that he wasn't very good in school. He does, however, have a great gift of intuition. He can sense what will make people smile. He knows, but cannot explain in words, what makes people laugh.

AT THE AGE of seventeen a poor boy arrived in the city of Philadelphia. He was hungry and tired and had no place to sleep.

This boy, who grew up to become a very great man, only went to school for two years. Then he began to study on his own. He learned so much and developed so many skills, it is difficult to name them all.

He was a writer and a reader, a printer and a teacher. He composed fine music and learned to play the harp, violin, and guitar. He was a scientist and inventor and also an expert swimmer. He worked as a postmaster and public official. He was a philosopher, debater, and public speaker, and he became a great statesman. He also spoke several languages. Have you guessed who he might be? Benjamin Franklin was his name.

Ben Franklin is an example of a great man who had highly developed both his right and left brains. He was a verbal, logical, and orderly man; but, was also creative, artistic, and imaginative.

For many years, scientists have believed that people were generally using only about ten percent of their brain. Today, many brain researchers are saying that most of us use only about two percent of our brain power.

The test in chapter three probably gave you an idea of your brain preference. Was it toward the right or left, or was it nearly equal? If you have a strong preference for one side, there are many things you can do to better develop the other side. If you are fairly well-balanced in brain function, you, too, can put your brain to better use. No matter how strong our brains are, we can always develop them further.

You may find it hard to believe that you have the same basic thinking equipment as Benjamin Franklin or Leonardo da Vinci, but you do. The difference is not in the size of your brain, it is in the way you use it. There are many examples of "great minds" who were, or are, skilled at using both hemispheres very well. The rest of us are likely to let the side take over that seems most comfortable and natural to us.

Your brain is very powerful and it becomes stronger and stronger with practice. Don't let those mighty powers of your brain go to waste.

Perhaps one reason President Ronald Reagan was elected to high offices is his ability to use in his speeches a style that appealed to both the right and left brain. Each speech usually contained concrete examples of facts and figures, wit and humor, stories of interest, and visual aids to explain his plans.

Education in our schools has, in the past, dealt mainly with left-brained subjects (reading, writing, spelling, speaking, and math calculations). It wouldn't be surprising if you have a left-brained preference, for you have probably had more practice with that side. Your left brain can get very tired and have what is called a "mental block" if you don't switch from time to time into right-brain activities.

GAIL AND MIKE were doing their homework at the kitchen table. Gail was working on a long list of science questions. At first, the answers came easily and then all of a sudden, Gail felt her mind go blank. "Mike, I just can't seem to remember some of the things we learned in school today," she said. Gail was having a "mental block."

Mike gave her some advice. "Mrs. Bell, our teacher this year, has given us ideas of what to do when our minds go blank. She often has us stop our work and do a few exercises or something creative. You can do something like that now for a few minutes. Then when you come back to do your homework, you'll probably find it easier. Mrs. Bell told us that this is a way for using the right brain to help break a left brain mental block."

MANY SCHOOLS do not realize the importance of the skill of intuition ("I don't know how to prove it; I just know it," said Roy.). Teachers have either discouraged it or ignored intuition. Yet, intuition is very necessary to develop creative ideas. Perhaps it is the key ingredient for success in all areas; in school, family life, and your future career. It is a very important part of making decisions and solving problems.

Although most schools do not encourage it, some students seem to have a natural ability for intuition. They

think with *both* halves of their brains fairly equally. They may not be encouraged or understood by their teachers, but these students often stand out as being highly creative.

"IF YOU DON'T finish your art assignment, you can't go to your math class."

"Until we finish playing this baseball game, none of you will be allowed to go to your English class."

WHEN WAS the last time you ever heard a teacher say something like that? Probably never. Art, music, physical education, and recess have always been thought of as "extras." They were often considered fun, but not really necessary. Not so. Art, music, and P.E. are necessary for right brain development.

Many teachers are aware of these ideas of educating the "whole brain." They use methods in their classrooms to help your two brains form a more perfect partnership. They know that short work sessions spaced widely apart are better than long sessions closer together. They bring into the classroom such things as simple relaxation exercises. They use many diagrams, pictures, films, and demonstrations. Teachers also know that it is better for students to take part in a new activity rather than watch or listen to someone else. Who knows, maybe some teachers will even set aside a time and place for daydreaming. Daydreaming is another activity that has always been greatly discouraged in the classroom. But, it, like intuition, is another important right brain creative skill.

"JANICE, WAKE UP" said the teacher. "You are supposed to be working on your science test."

Janice opened her eyes. "I'm not sleeping" she said. "I'm just putting myself into a right brain mood. I read that if you do that first, you'll probably do better on a test."

Janice was right, of course. However, don't try closing your eyes in class for very long unless you know you have a teacher who understands what you are doing and will encourage such actions. (And don't use it as an excuse to take a nap.) You don't need to spend much time switching to the right hemisphere. Just a few seconds or a minute will do. There are ways of doing this that will not be noticeable to anyone but you.

Suppose you are in the classroom ready to take a social studies test and you are uptight about it. You seem to have a mental block. (The fear of an exam can cause stimulation of the sympathetic nerve in your body. This, in turn, can cause great body stress.) To overcome this stress, sit quietly, take some deep breaths. For a moment, let your mind wander into the past. Picture some of the things you have learned. Pretend that you are watching events in a motion picture. For example, if your test is on the American Revolution, picture an event such as the tea being dumped off the ships by men dressed as Native Americans. Now, switch from those right-brained mental pictures back to the test. Chances are your left and right brain will work together and you will remember many more answers to the test questions.

Do you ever get nervous before you must get up in front of the class? Do you get upset at the idea of giving an oral report? There are some ways to help yourself. Try deep breathing again. Take deep breaths until you feel your body relax. Let your mind think about the subject of your report. Try to picture in your mind illustrations of your talk as if you were choosing illustrations for a book.

Another helpful hint is to try to think of a time in your life when you had a successful experience (like winning a game, a prize, a contest). This will build up your confidence. When it is your turn, take another deep breath and walk to the front of the room with pride. Think to yourself, "I have studied this subject and probably know all I need to know to give a good report." This activity can also be very helpful before you take a test.

Both in the test and oral report situation, you have used relaxation and imagery. These are two important activities that make it possible for the right brain to help the left.

Michaelangelo, one of the greatest artists of all time, had superior powers of imagination and a highly developed right brain. He was talented as a sculptor, painter, poet, architect, and military engineer. His figures in sculpture and paintings look alive, truly human and filled with great strength. In order to achieve this technical success, the artist studied and analyzed the anatomy of the human body. To do this, he used the left brain analytical functions to help the artistic, creative right brain skills.

Walt Disney will be remembered as one of the most creative men of our time. His ideas, thoughts, and fantasies were used to produce some very imaginative movies. "Fantasia" and "Walt Disney's Wonderful World of Color" are good examples. Disneyland and Disneyworld, his "dream playgrounds," were also created from his marvelous imagination. Millions of people have enjoyed these "magic kingdoms." They are like trips into a world of daydreams. For his fantastic creations, Disney used a combination of the right brain functions with the left brain technical skills to make his dreams a reality.

Da Vinci's Aerial Screw *(an early helicopter)*

A LARGE red brick mansion is located on a hill in the ancient town of Amboise, France. Two American boys, Steve and Gary, were on a tour with their parents. They had found, in the basement of this old house, a fascinating display of models of scientific inventions.

"Gary, look at this neat helicopter and this strange looking airplane," exclaimed Steve.

"Yes, I saw those. They're really interesting, but look at these things over here. Check out this drawbridge. It really works. And look at this model. It looks like a submarine."

You may think these boys were looking at models of modern inventions, but not so. They were in the home of

Leonardo da Vinci. He had lived and worked here almost five hundred years ago. The models of his inventions were built and put here on display by the IBM Corporation. They are fairly large and each mounted on a platform or in a case. They include mechanical devices to be used for many purposes: Military, maritime (relating to the sea), hydraulic (movement of fluids or gasses), and aeronautical.

Leonardo da Vinci had creative ideas for mechanical inventions that really worked, inventions that were centuries ahead of their time. He, perhaps, is the *very* best example of a human being whose creations were the result of a highly developed right and left brain working together to the greatest degree.

Da Vinci was not only an inventor, but a great artist, too. His most famous paintings are "The Last Supper" and "The Mona Lisa." He is often considered the most outstanding creator, artist, thinker, inventor of all time.

SOME PEOPLE would like to go through life just painting pictures, dancing, listening to music, and taking part in sports activities. They might prefer to use intuition rather than logic and spend the rest of their time daydreaming.

This may sound fun, but do you think that would be the answer to their life's problems? Most of the subjects we study, to prepare us for life, require learning facts. There is a great need for the left brain skills. Speaking, writing, and reading skills are particularly important. And other left brain functions such as reasoning, analyzing, and categorizing, are also very important in our lives.

It is not enough to know what to think, we must also learn how to think. A skill called "critical thinking" is becoming very important as our world becomes more technical. Critical thinking is using your brain to make decisions.

These decisions can be based on logic (left brain) or intuition (right brain).

One aspect of critical thinking is problem solving. The right brain can be involved by showing the problem in pictures, diagrams, or graphs. The left brain comes up with sequences, categories, and logical steps. The right brain can picture creative answers to the problem. The left brain is needed to put these ideas into words or numbers.

Critical thinking is a perfect example of the cooperation of our two hemispheres. To do the best you can possibly do, you need to develop both your brains by learning to use each one to help the other. You can, and should, put your whole brain to work for you.

BIBLIOGRAPHY

BLAKESLEE, THOMAS R., *Right Brain*, Garden City, NY: Anchor Pr./Doubleday, 1980

BUZON, TONY, *Use Both Sides of Your Brain*, New York, NY: Dutton, 1983

BUZON, TONY, *The Brain Users Guide*, New York, NY: Dutton, 1983

DOWNEY, BILL, *Right Brain . . . Write On!*, Englewood Cliffs, NJ: Prentice, 1984

EDWARDS, BETTY, *Drawing on the Right Side of the Brain*, Los Angeles, CA: Tarcher, 1979

FACKLAM, MARJORIE AND FACKLAM, HOWARD, *The Brain*, San Diego, CA: Harcourt, 1982

GILLING, DICK AND BRIGHTWELL, ROBERT, *The Human Brain*, New York, NY: Facts on File, 1983

HAINES, GAIL K., *Brain Power*, New York, NY: Watts, 1979

MCNAMARA, LOUISE G. AND LITCHFIELD, ADA B., *Your Busy Brain*, New York, NY: Little, 1973

NOONE, RICHARD, *In Search of the Dream People*, New York, NY: Morrow, 1972

KETTLEKAMP, LARRY, *The Dreaming Mind*, New York, NY: Macmillan, 1975

LINDSAY, RAE, *The Left-Handed Book*, New York, NY: Watts, 1980

SILVERSTEIN, ALVIN, *The Left-Hander's World*, Chicago, IL: Follett, 1977

SIMON, S. AND KENDRICK, D., *About Your Brain*, New York, NY: McGraw, 1981

SHARP, PAT, *Brain Power*, New York, NY: Lothrop, 1984

SPRINGER, SALLY P. AND DEUTSCH, GEORGE, *Left Brain, Right Brain*, New York, NY: W. H. Freeman, 1981

VITALE, BARBARA MEISTER, *Unicorns Are Real*, Rolling Hills Estates, CA: Jalmar, 1984

WARD, BRIAN, *The Brain and Nervous System*, New York, NY: Watts, 1981

WONDER, JACQUELYN AND DONOVAN, PRICILLA, *Whole Brain Thinking*, New York, NY: Morrow, 1984

ZDENEK, MARILEE, *The Right Brain Experience*, New York, NY: McGraw, 1983

GLOSSARY

ANALYTICAL—Examining an idea or a thing in detail by breaking it into parts.

ANATOMY—The internal and external structure of the body and its parts.

AVERAGE—The normal or typical kind.

CELL—A small basic unit of living matter.

CEREBELLUM—The part of the brain that coordinates the activities of the muscles.

CEREBRUM—The part of the brain that controls voluntary movements and mental activities.

COMMUNICATION—The transfer of information, such as facts, ideas, or emotions.

CORPUS CALLOSUM—The part of the brain that separates the left from the right hemisphere.

CREATIVE—Able to bring into being, cause to exist.

CULTURE—The ideas and way of life of certain people at a certain time.

EPILEPSY—A disorder of the brain and nervous system.

EPILEPTIC SEIZURE—A sudden attack of tightening of the muscles that may cause convulsions and fainting.

FANTASIES—Thoughts, ideas, and daydreams brought about by the use of the creative imagination.

GENIUS—A person with outstanding mental powers and creative ability.

HEMISPHERE—Either half of a symmetrical object whose shape is roughly that of a sphere (a ball, a globe, the brain, and so on).

HYGIENE—A system of rules for keeping healthy and preventing disease.

INHERIT—To have or get certain characteristics or traits from parents or ancestors.

INTUITION—The power of knowing something without having to reason it out.

MOLECULE—A particle of matter made up of two or more atoms joined by a pair of shared electrons.

MONOTONE—Words or sounds said with no change in pitch.

MORAL—The lesson taught by a story or fable.

NERVE—A bundle of fibers carrying impulses between the brain and other parts of the body.

NERVOUS SYSTEM—The bodily system that includes the brain, spinal cord, and nerves, and that receives and interprets "messages" from stimuli and transmits "instructions" to the body.

NEURON—The basic unit of the nervous system consisting of a cell body and its fibers.

PARALYZED—Having lost the power to move or feel in a part or parts of the body.

PREFERENCE—A liking for someone or something over another.

RECEPTOR—A nerve ending that receives various signals or messages which it transmits to the brain through the nervous system.

SPATIAL—Of, like, or involving spaces.

STROKE—The sudden severe attack of illness as of paralysis, frequently associated with a rupture or obstruction of an artery of the brain.

TECHNIQUE—A system or method for accomplishing a task.

UNIQUE—Being the only one of its kind.

VERBAL—Relating to or made up of words.